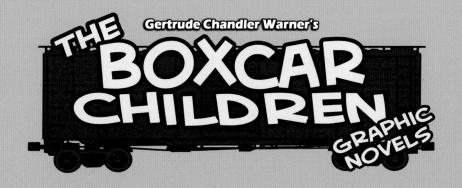

# Gertrude Chandler Warner's
# THE BOXCAR CHILDREN GRAPHIC NOVELS

## BOOK FIFTEEN
## MOUNTAIN TOP MYSTERY

Henry, Jessie, Violet, and Benny Alden are going to climb a mountain! The hike up Old Flat Top is only supposed to take a day, but a dangerous rockslide changes everything. The rockslide reveals a hidden cave that just may hold a legendary treasure. Can the Boxcar Children solve the mystery of what's on top of the mountain?

# THE BOXCAR CHILDREN
## GRAPHIC NOVELS

1. THE BOXCAR CHILDREN
2. SURPRISE ISLAND
3. THE YELLOW HOUSE MYSTERY
4. MYSTERY RANCH
5. MIKE'S MYSTERY
6. BLUE BAY MYSTERY
7. SNOWBOUND MYSTERY
8. TREE HOUSE MYSTERY
9. THE HAUNTED CABIN MYSTERY
10. THE AMUSEMENT PARK MYSTERY
11. THE PIZZA MYSTERY
12. THE CASTLE MYSTERY
13. THE WOODSHED MYSTERY
14. THE LIGHTHOUSE MYSTERY
15. MOUNTAIN TOP MYSTERY
16. HOUSEBOAT MYSTERY
17. BICYCLE MYSTERY
18. MYSTERY IN THE SAND

Gertrude Chandler Warner's

# THE BOXCAR CHILDREN
## MOUNTAIN TOP MYSTERY

Adapted by Joeming Dunn
Illustrated by Ben Dunn

Henry Alden

Watch

Jessie Alden

Violet Alden

Benny Alden

magic
wagon

**visit us at www.abdopublishing.com**

Published by Magic Wagon, a division of the ABDO Group, 8000 West 78th Street, Edina, Minnesota 55439. Copyright © 2011 by Abdo Consulting Group, Inc. International copyrights reserved in all countries. All rights reserved. No part of this book may be reproduced in any form without written permission from the publisher.

Graphic Planet™ is a trademark and logo of Magic Wagon.

This edition produced by arrangement with Albert Whitman & Company. THE BOXCAR CHILDREN is a registered trademark of Albert Whitman & Company. www.albertwhitman.com

Printed in the United States of America, North Mankato, Minnesota.
092010
012011
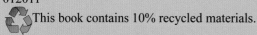This book contains 10% recycled materials.

Adapted by Joeming Dunn
Illustrated by Ben Dunn
Colored by Robby Bevard
Lettered by Joeming Dunn & Doug Dlin
Edited by Stephanie Hedlund
Interior layout and design by Kristen Fitzner Denton
Cover art by Ben Dunn

**Library of Congress Cataloging-in-Publication Data**

Dunn, Joeming W.
  Mountain top mystery / adapted by Joeming Dunn ; illustrated by Ben Dunn.
     p. cm. --  (Boxcar children graphic novels)
  At head of title: Gertrude Chandler Warner's The Boxcar children.
  "Graphic Planet"--Copyright p.
  ISBN 978-1-61641-123-7
  1.  Graphic novels. [1. Graphic novels. 2. Mystery and detective stories. 3. Mountains--Fiction. 4. Brothers and sisters--Fiction. 5. Orphans--Fiction. 6. Warner, Gertrude Chandler, 1890-1979. Mountain top mystery--Adaptations.]  I. Dunn, Ben, ill. II. Warner, Gertrude Chandler, 1890-1979. Mountain top mystery. III. Title.
  PZ7.7.D86Mo 2011
  741.5'973--dc22
                                                                      2010016149

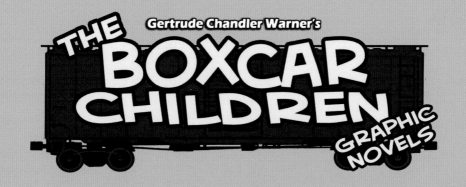

BOOK FIFTEEN

# MOUNTAIN TOP MYSTERY

## Contents

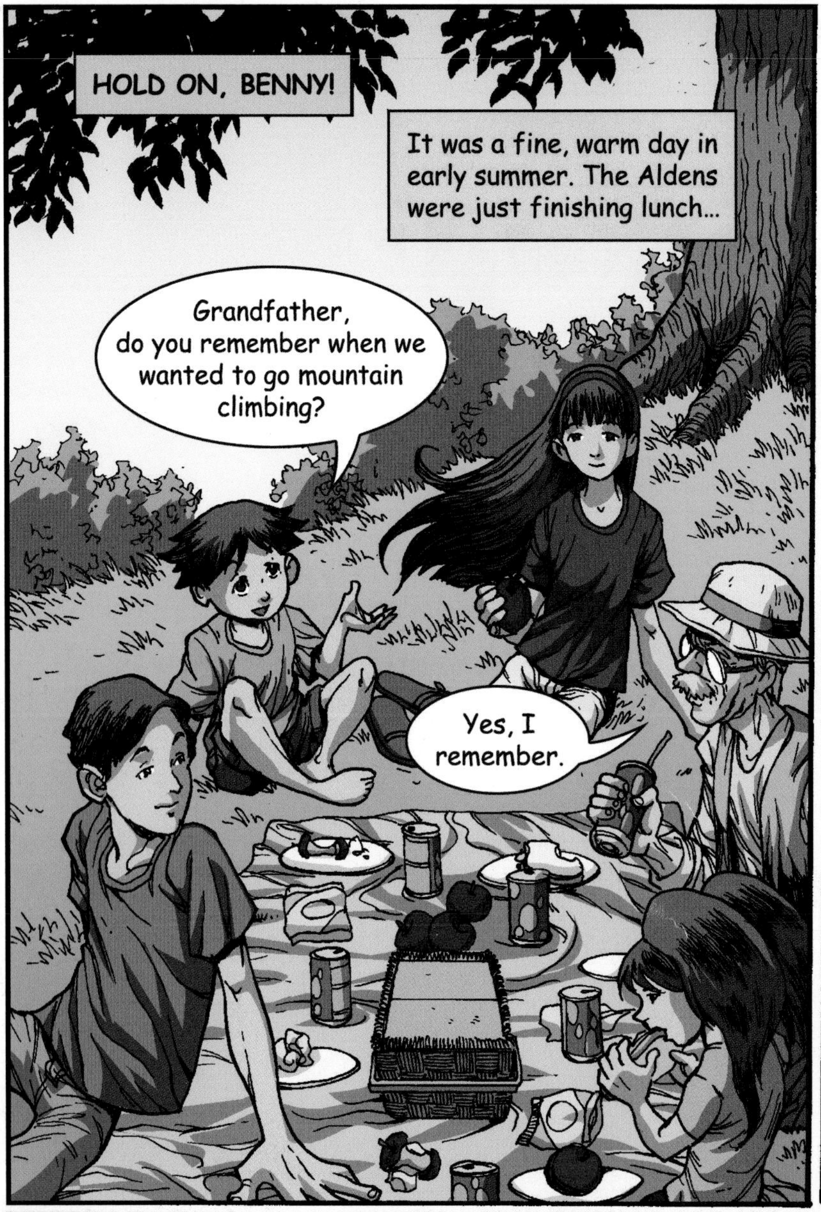
HOLD ON, BENNY!
It was a fine, warm day in early summer. The Aldens were just finishing lunch...
Grandfather, do you remember when we wanted to go mountain climbing?
Yes, I remember.

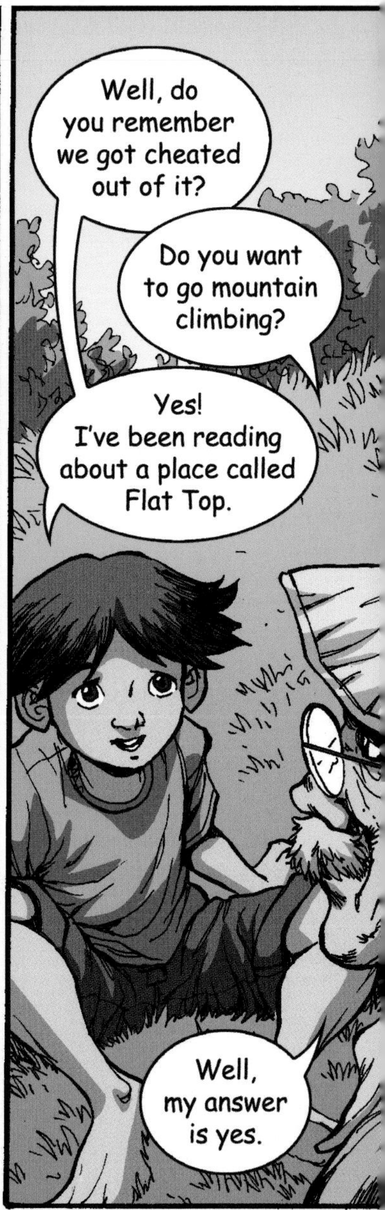
Well, do you remember we got cheated out of it?
Do you want to go mountain climbing?
Yes! I've been reading about a place called Flat Top.
Well, my answer is yes.

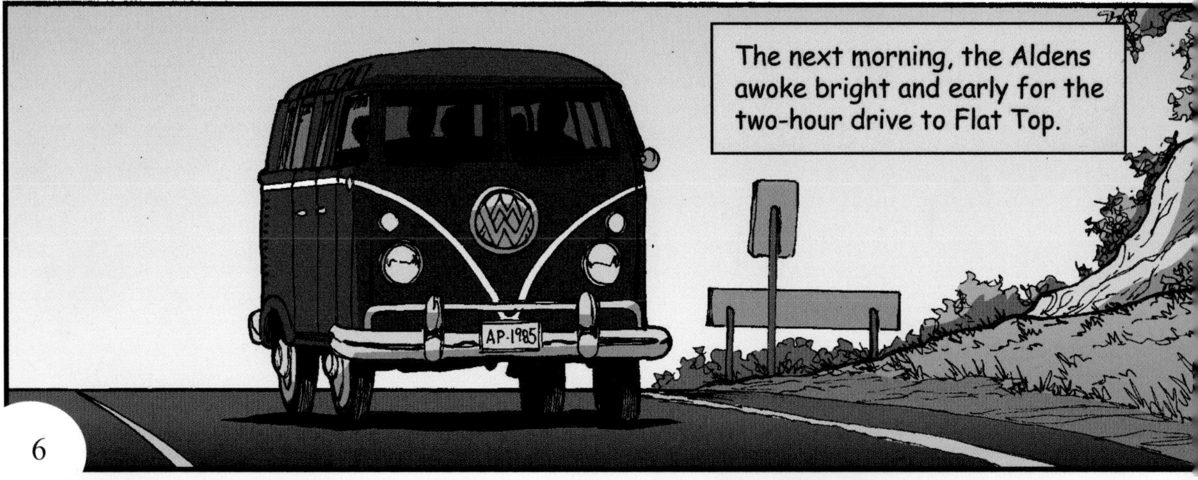
The next morning, the Aldens awoke bright and early for the two-hour drive to Flat Top.
AP-1985

Oh, isn't this lovely?

That's Old Flat Top.

PARK 2 m

They soon arrived at the country store at the base of the mountain.

Granny's COUNTRY STORE

POST OFFICE

At the store, the Aldens got everything they needed for the climb.

TTOP ATIONAL PARK

The path is well marked, and there's only one. It's also the path down.

NATL
RULES
• DO NOT FEE
• STAY ON T
• NO FIRES

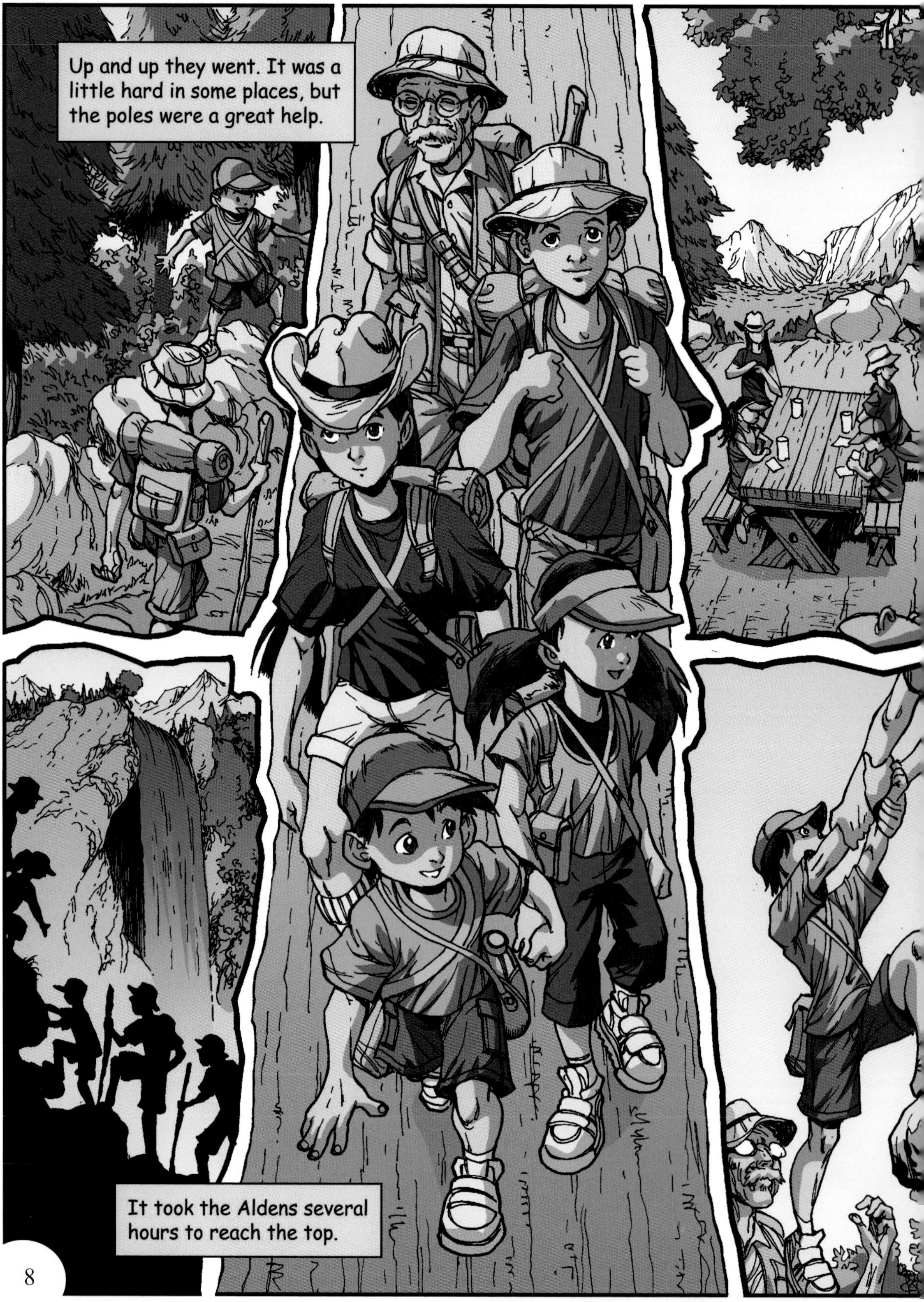
Up and up they went. It was a little hard in some places, but the poles were a great help.
It took the Aldens several hours to reach the top.

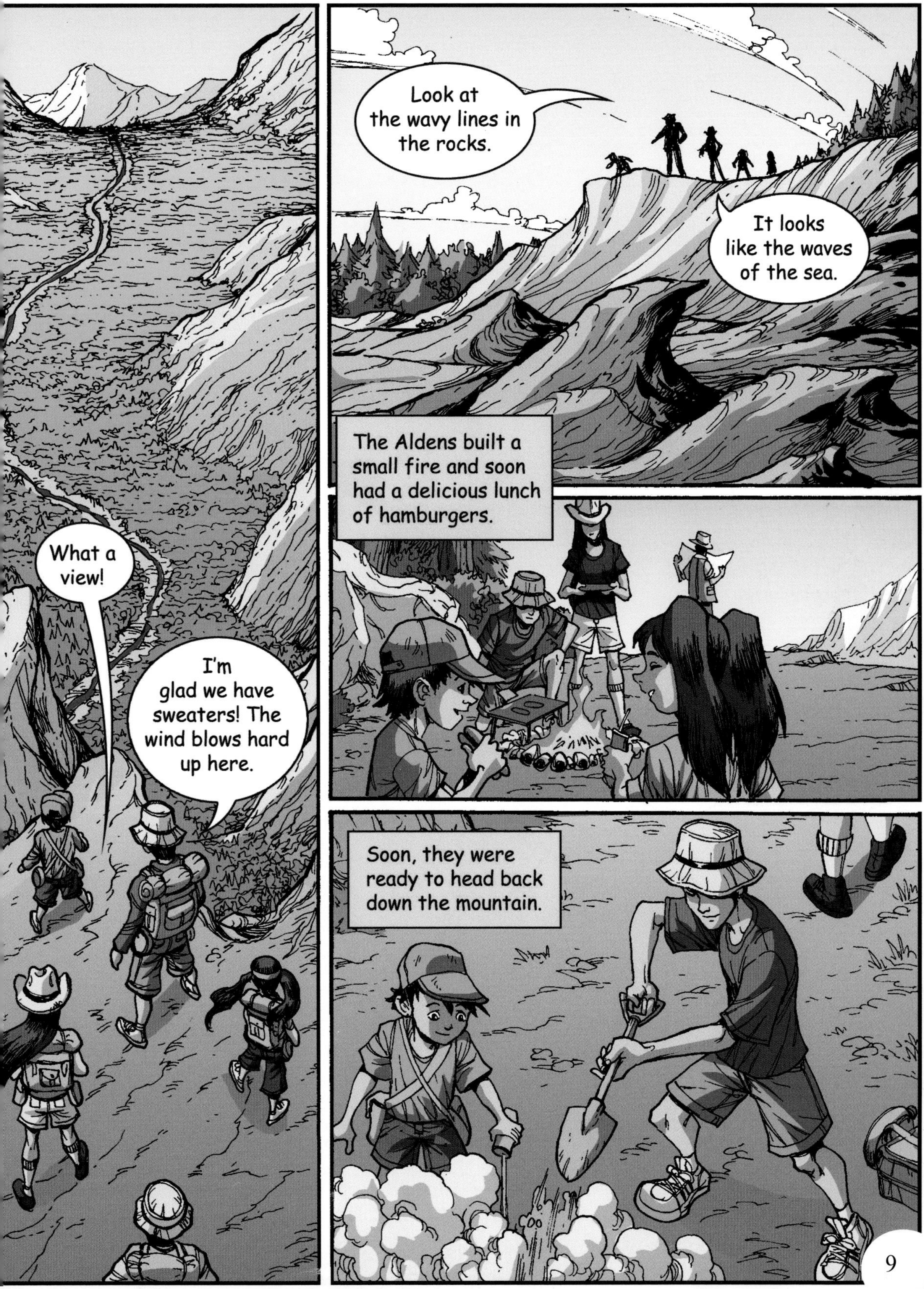
What a view!
I'm glad we have sweaters! The wind blows hard up here.
Look at the wavy lines in the rocks.
It looks like the waves of the sea.
The Aldens built a small fire and soon had a delicious lunch of hamburgers.
Soon, they were ready to head back down the mountain.

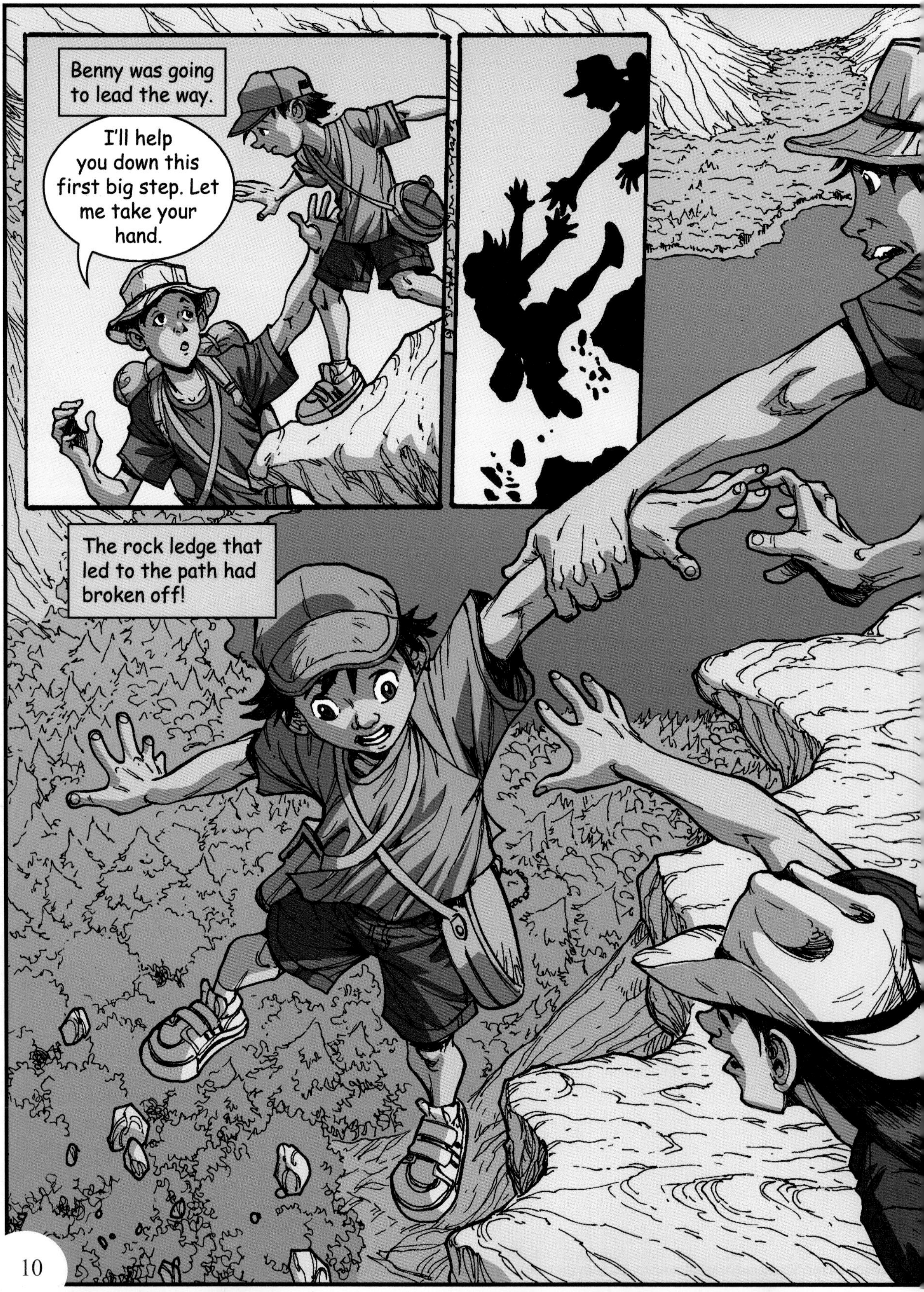
Benny was going to lead the way.
I'll help you down this first big step. Let me take your hand.
The rock ledge that led to the path had broken off!

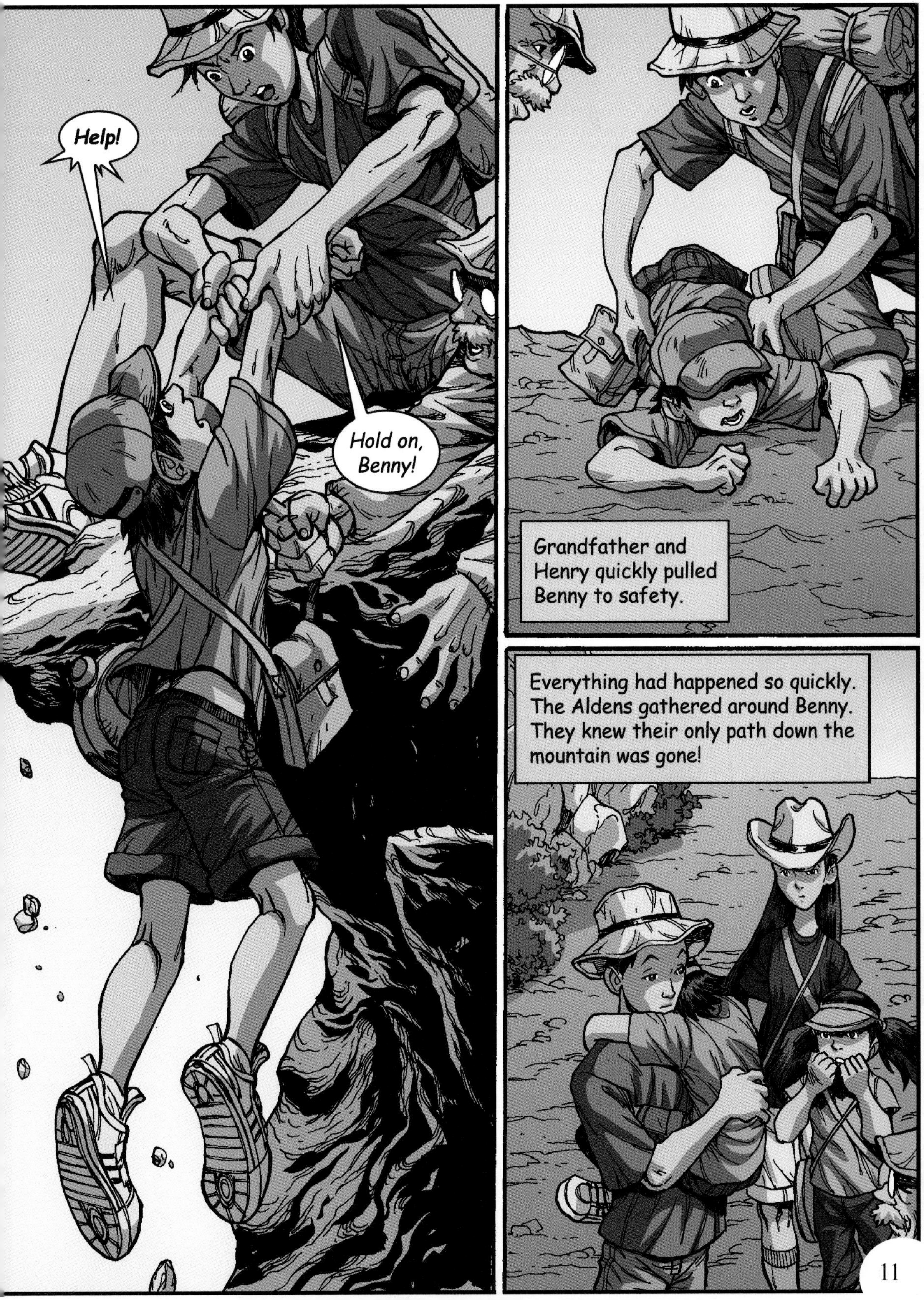

Help!
Hold on, Benny!
Grandfather and Henry quickly pulled Benny to safety.
Everything had happened so quickly. The Aldens gathered around Benny. They knew their only path down the mountain was gone!

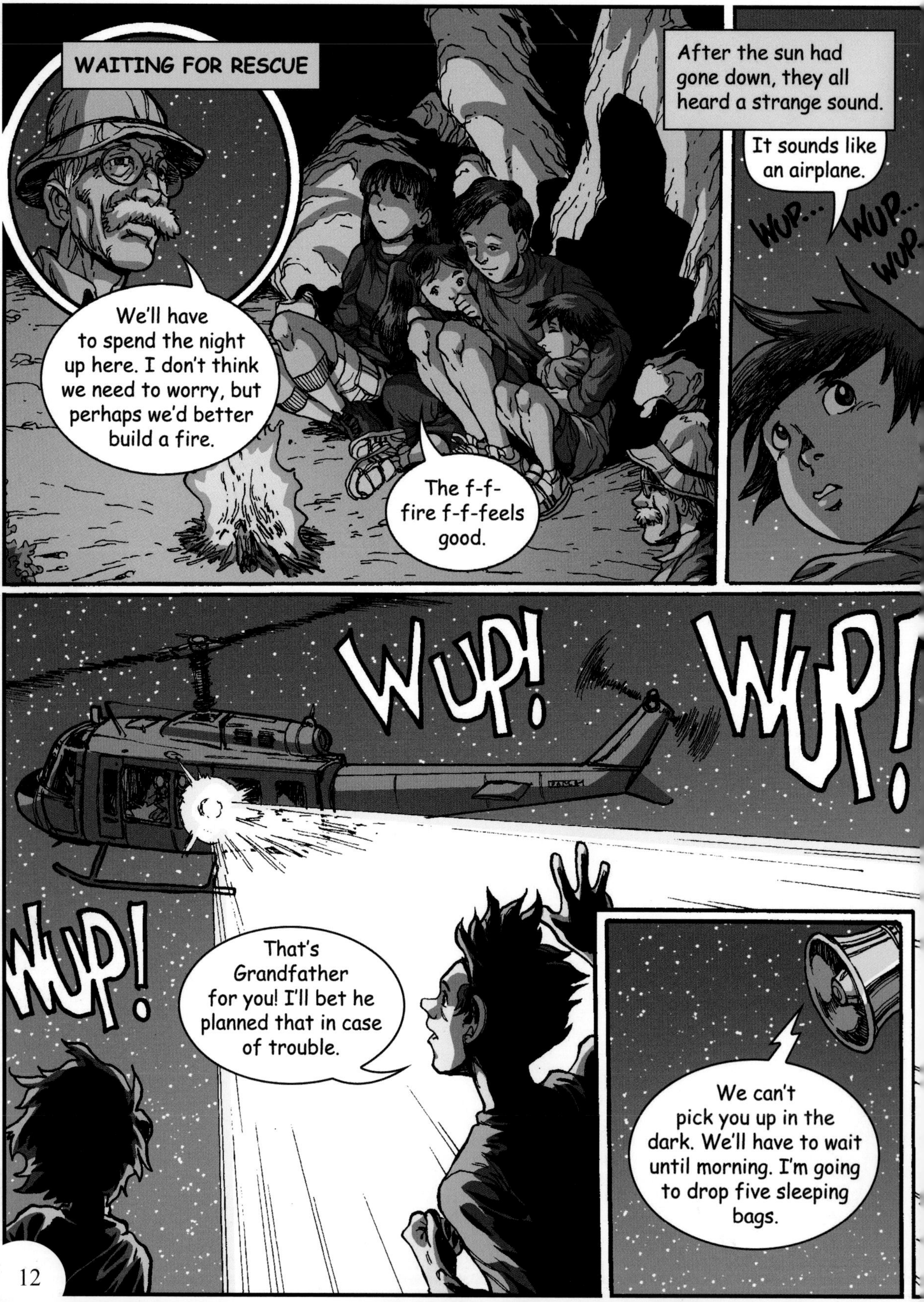
WAITING FOR RESCUE
We'll have to spend the night up here. I don't think we need to worry, but perhaps we'd better build a fire.
The f-f-fire f-f-feels good.
After the sun had gone down, they all heard a strange sound.
It sounds like an airplane.
WUP... WUP... WUP...
WUP! WUP!
WUP!
That's Grandfather for you! I'll bet he planned that in case of trouble.
We can't pick you up in the dark. We'll have to wait until morning. I'm going to drop five sleeping bags.

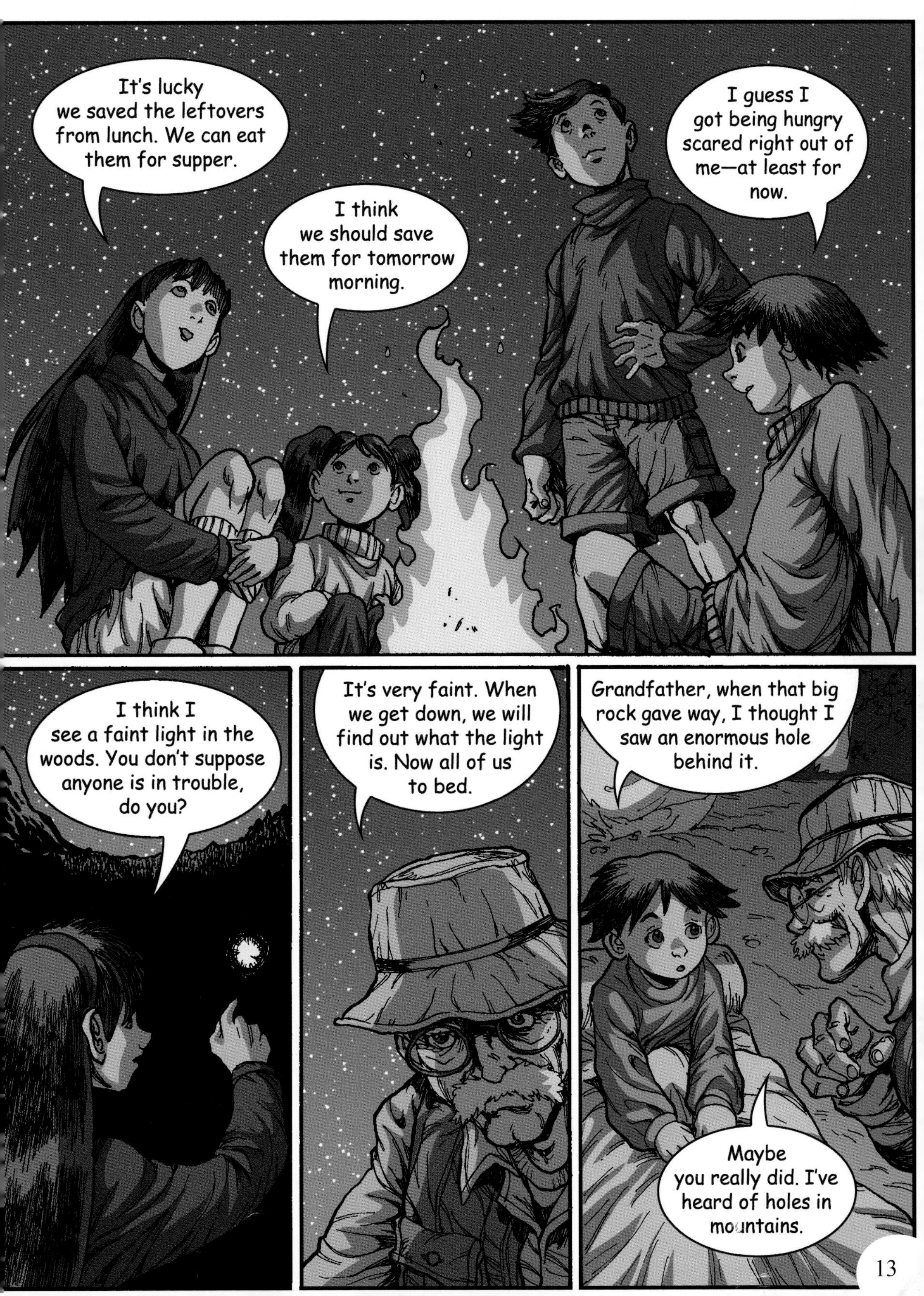

It's lucky we saved the leftovers from lunch. We can eat them for supper.
I think we should save them for tomorrow morning.
I guess I got being hungry scared right out of me—at least for now.
I think I see a faint light in the woods. You don't suppose anyone is in trouble, do you?
It's very faint. When we get down, we will find out what the light is. Now all of us to bed.
Grandfather, when that big rock gave way, I thought I saw an enormous hole behind it.
Maybe you really did. I've heard of holes in mountains.

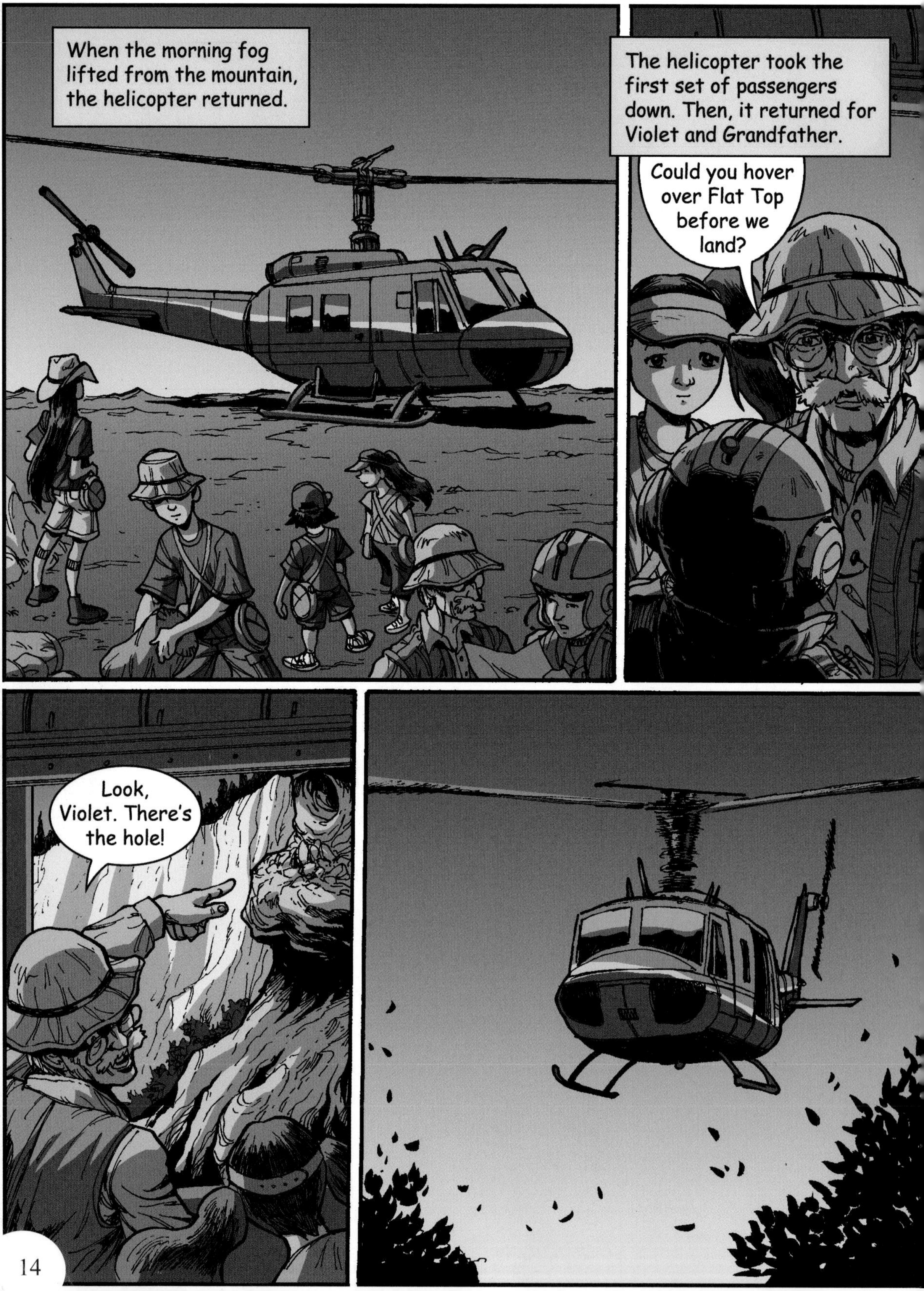
When the morning fog lifted from the mountain, the helicopter returned.
The helicopter took the first set of passengers down. Then, it returned for Violet and Grandfather.
Could you hover over Flat Top before we land?
Look, Violet. There's the hole!

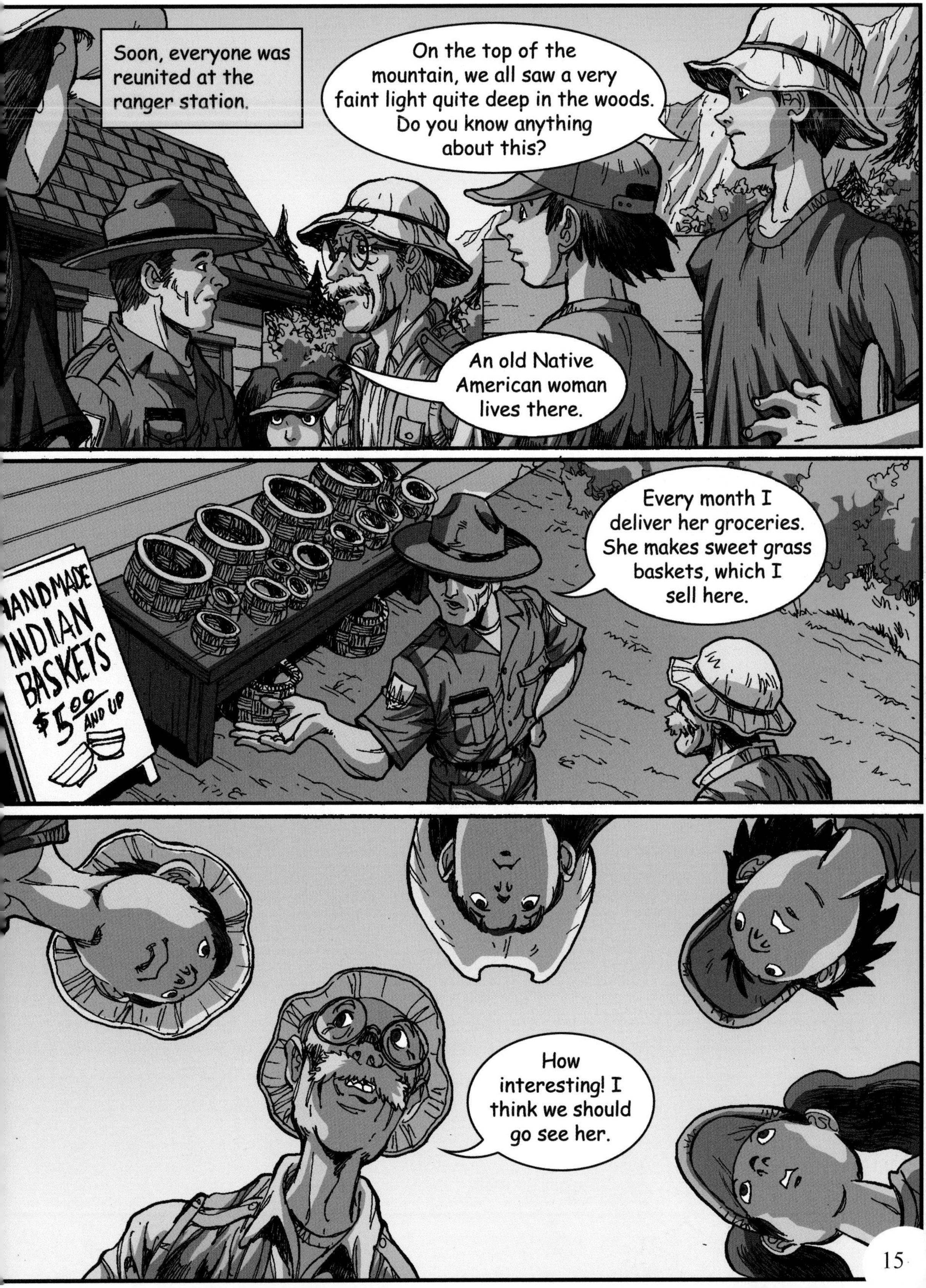

Soon, everyone was reunited at the ranger station.
On the top of the mountain, we all saw a very faint light quite deep in the woods. Do you know anything about this?
An old Native American woman lives there.
HANDMADE INDIAN BASKETS $5.00 AND UP
Every month I deliver her groceries. She makes sweet grass baskets, which I sell here.
How interesting! I think we should go see her.

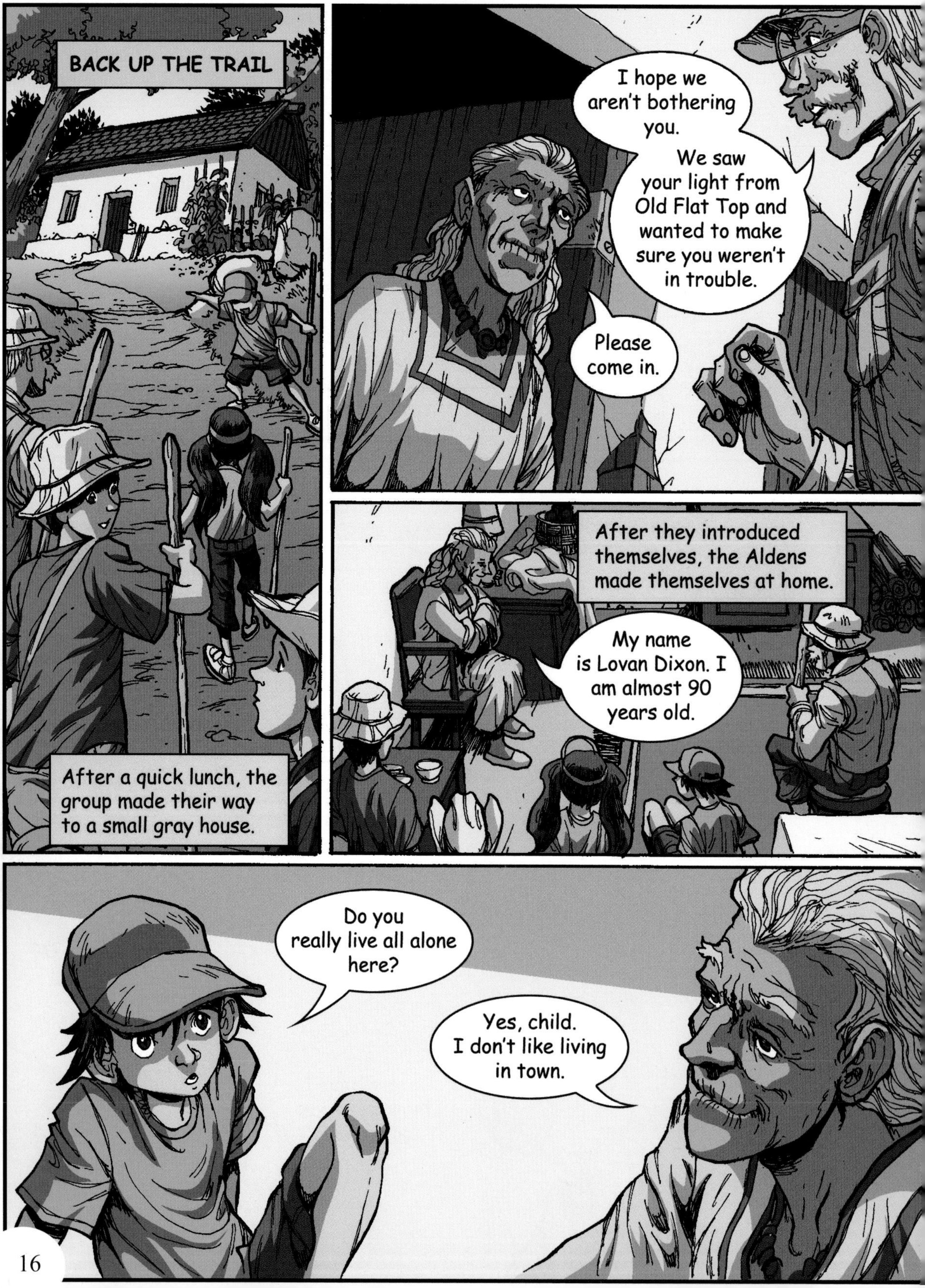
BACK UP THE TRAIL
After a quick lunch, the group made their way to a small gray house.
I hope we aren't bothering you.
We saw your light from Old Flat Top and wanted to make sure you weren't in trouble.
Please come in.
After they introduced themselves, the Aldens made themselves at home.
My name is Lovan Dixon. I am almost 90 years old.
Do you really live all alone here?
Yes, child. I don't like living in town.

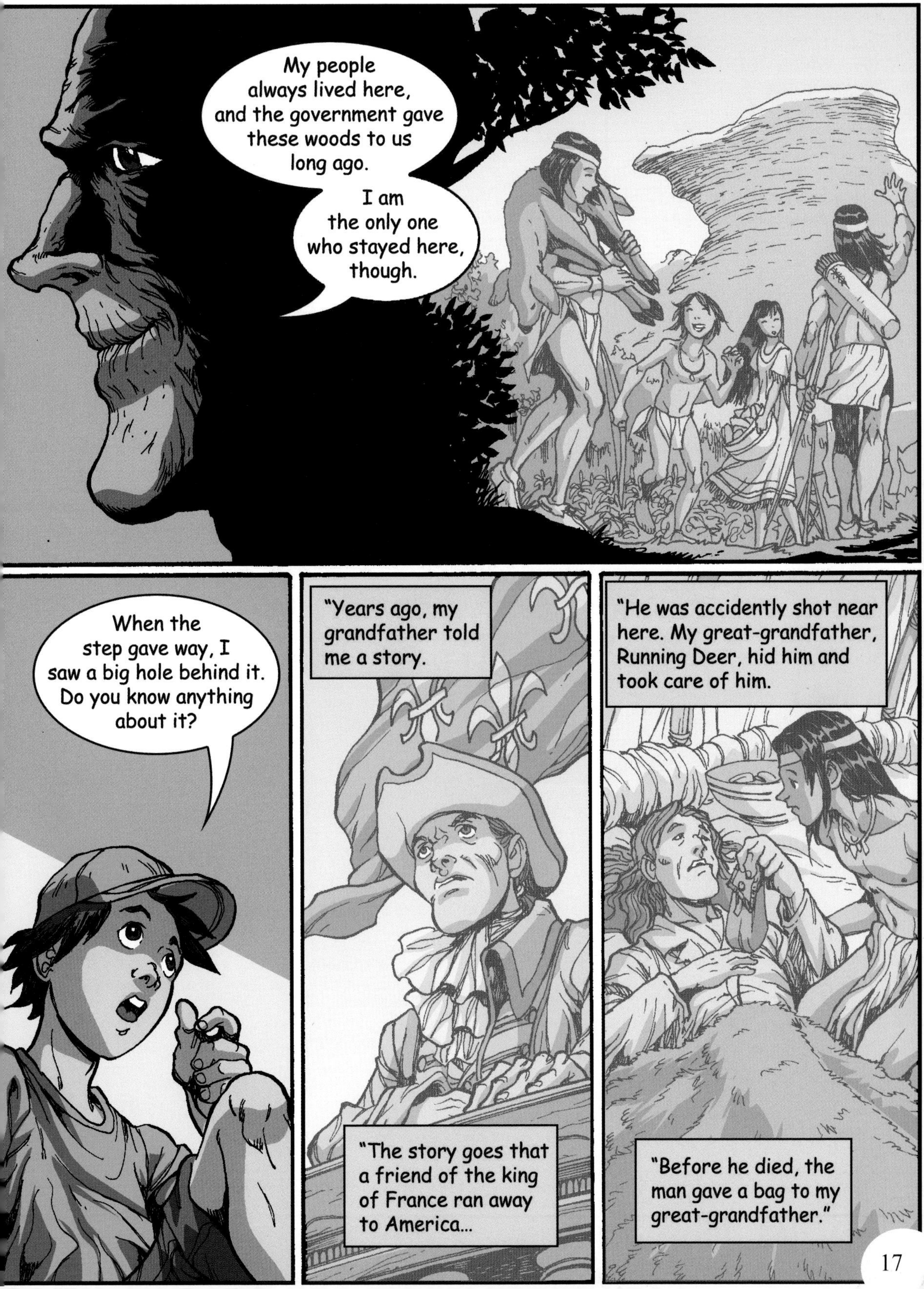

My people always lived here, and the government gave these woods to us long ago.
I am the only one who stayed here, though.
When the step gave way, I saw a big hole behind it. Do you know anything about it?
"Years ago, my grandfather told me a story.
"The story goes that a friend of the king of France ran away to America...
"He was accidently shot near here. My great-grandfather, Running Deer, hid him and took care of him.
"Before he died, the man gave a bag to my great-grandfather."

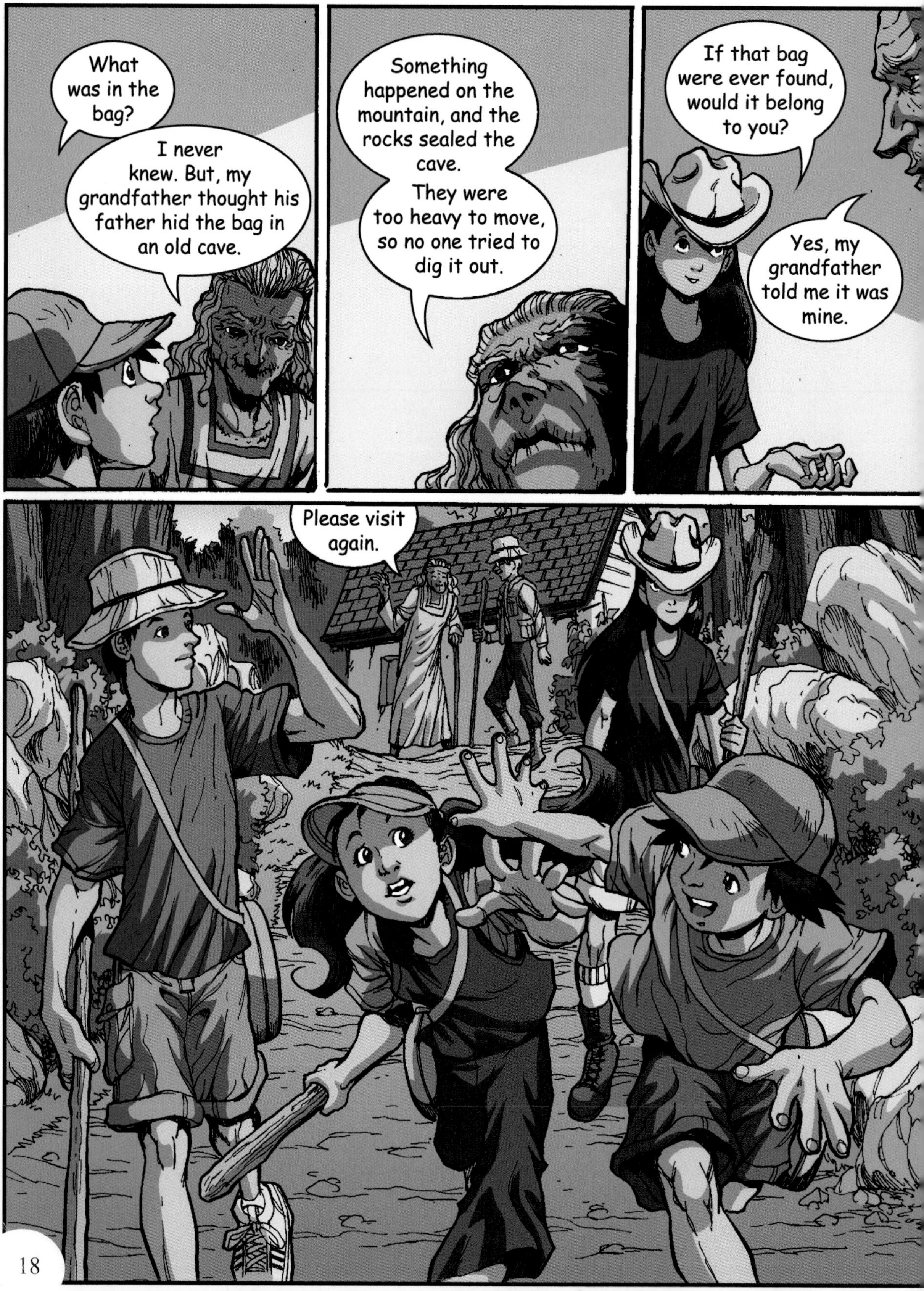
What was in the bag?
I never knew. But, my grandfather thought his father hid the bag in an old cave.
Something happened on the mountain, and the rocks sealed the cave.
They were too heavy to move, so no one tried to dig it out.
If that bag were ever found, would it belong to you?
Yes, my grandfather told me it was mine.
Please visit again.

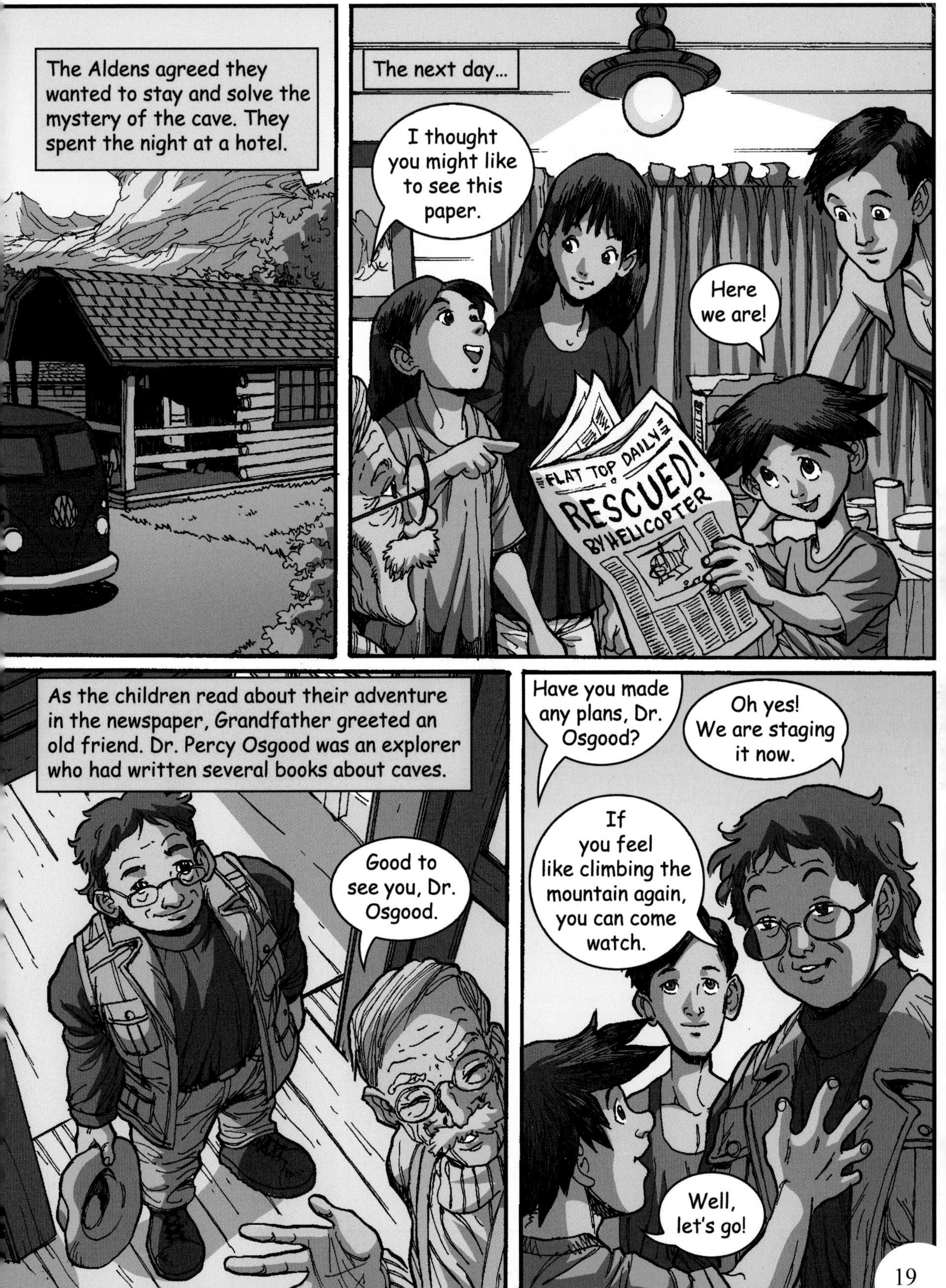
The Aldens agreed they wanted to stay and solve the mystery of the cave. They spent the night at a hotel.
The next day...
I thought you might like to see this paper.
Here we are!
FLAT TOP DAILY
RESCUED!
BY HELICOPTER
As the children read about their adventure in the newspaper, Grandfather greeted an old friend. Dr. Percy Osgood was an explorer who had written several books about caves.
Good to see you, Dr. Osgood.
Have you made any plans, Dr. Osgood?
Oh yes! We are staging it now.
If you feel like climbing the mountain again, you can come watch.
Well, let's go!

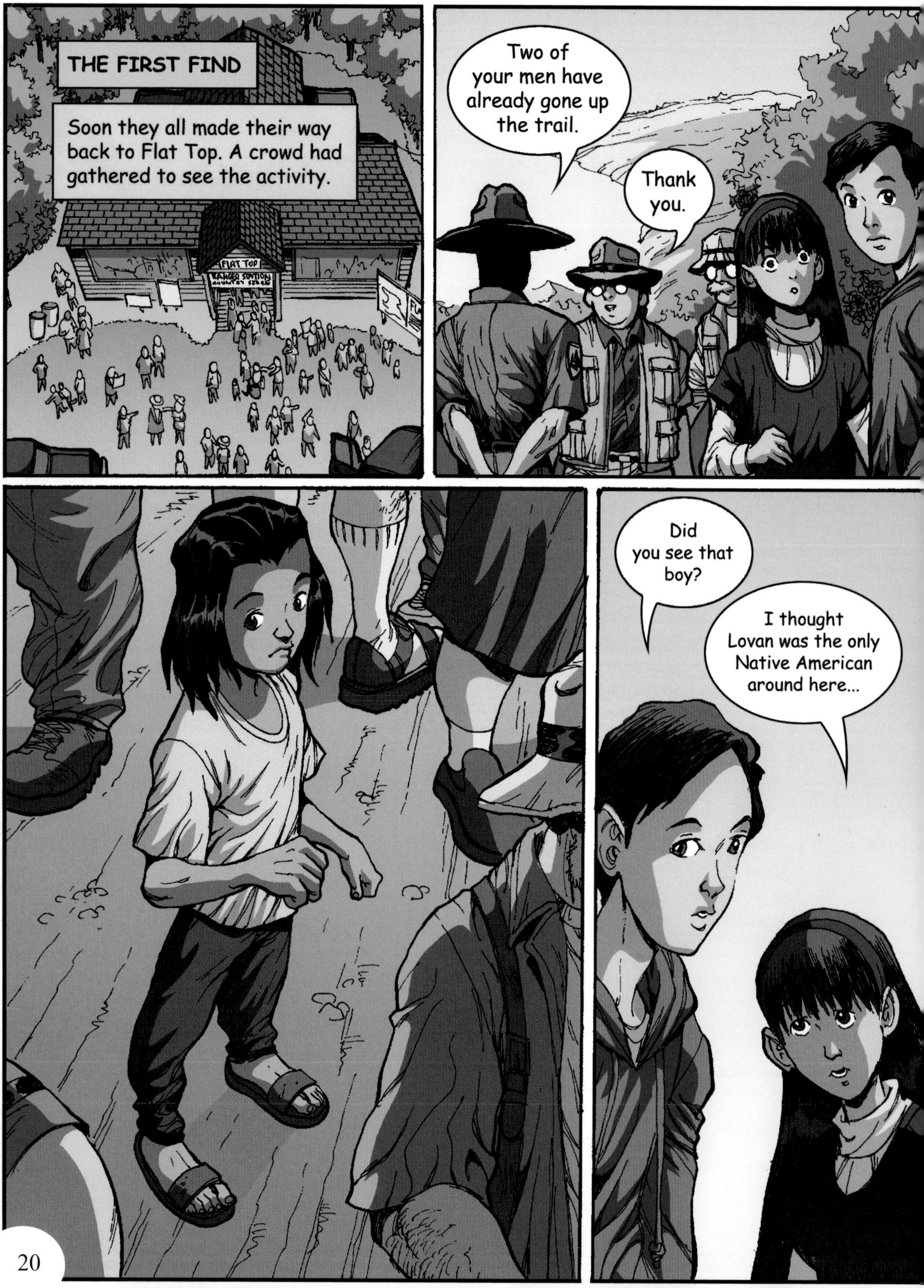
THE FIRST FIND
Soon they all made their way back to Flat Top. A crowd had gathered to see the activity.
FLAT TOP
RANGER STATION
Two of your men have already gone up the trail.
Thank you.
Did you see that boy?
I thought Lovan was the only Native American around here...

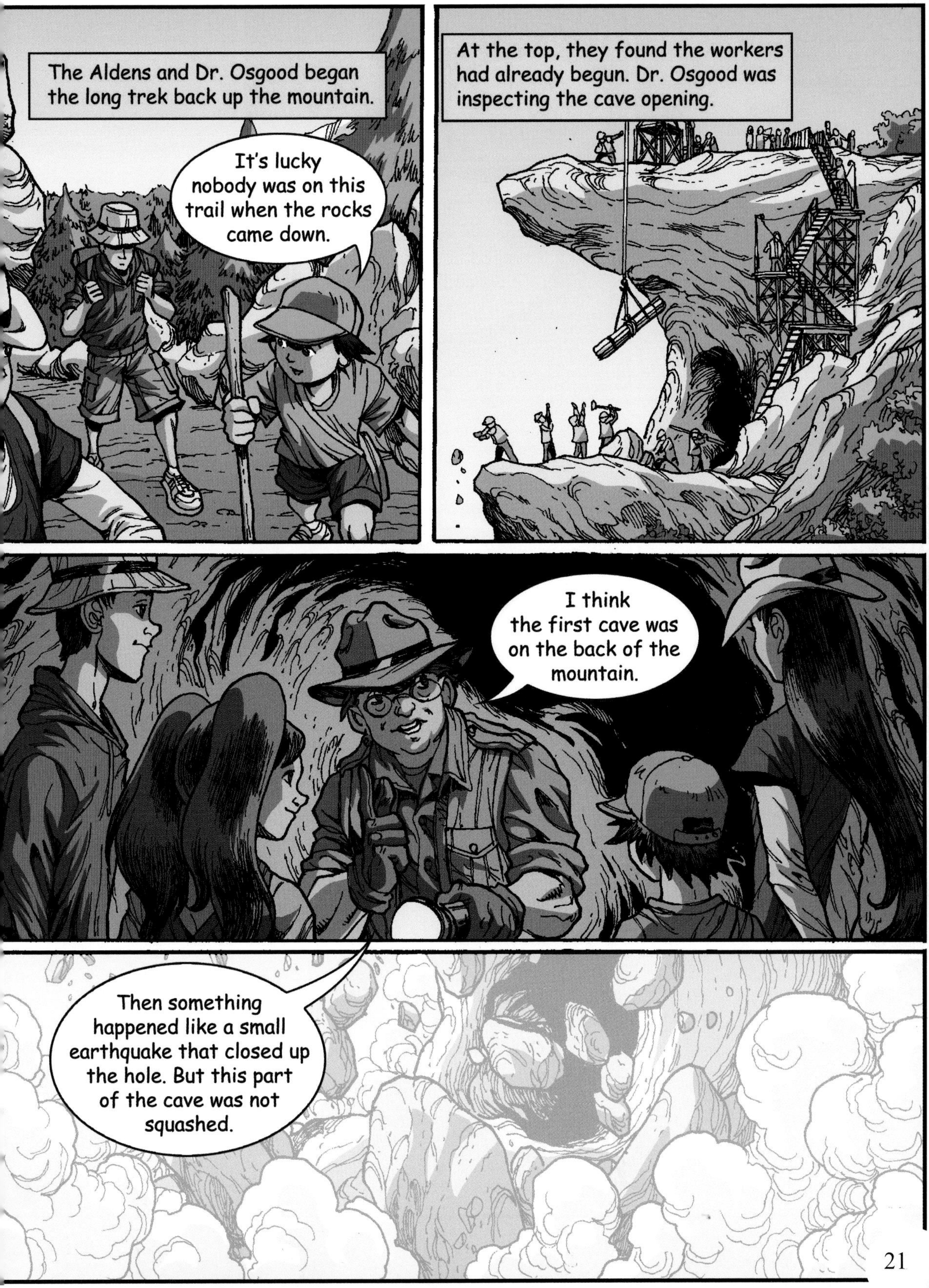

The Aldens and Dr. Osgood began the long trek back up the mountain.
It's lucky nobody was on this trail when the rocks came down.
At the top, they found the workers had already begun. Dr. Osgood was inspecting the cave opening.
I think the first cave was on the back of the mountain.
Then something happened like a small earthquake that closed up the hole. But this part of the cave was not squashed.

Then this front hole is really the back of the cave.

Right!

What did you see in the cave?

The hole grows larger. If we crawled in about 15 feet, we could actually stand up.

Have you found something already?

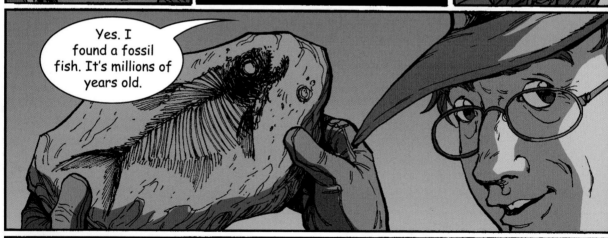

Yes. I found a fossil fish. It's millions of years old.

Yes, and this is the proof.

Does that mean that once this mountain was under water?

After showing the Aldens what he found, Dr. Osgood led them back out of the cave.

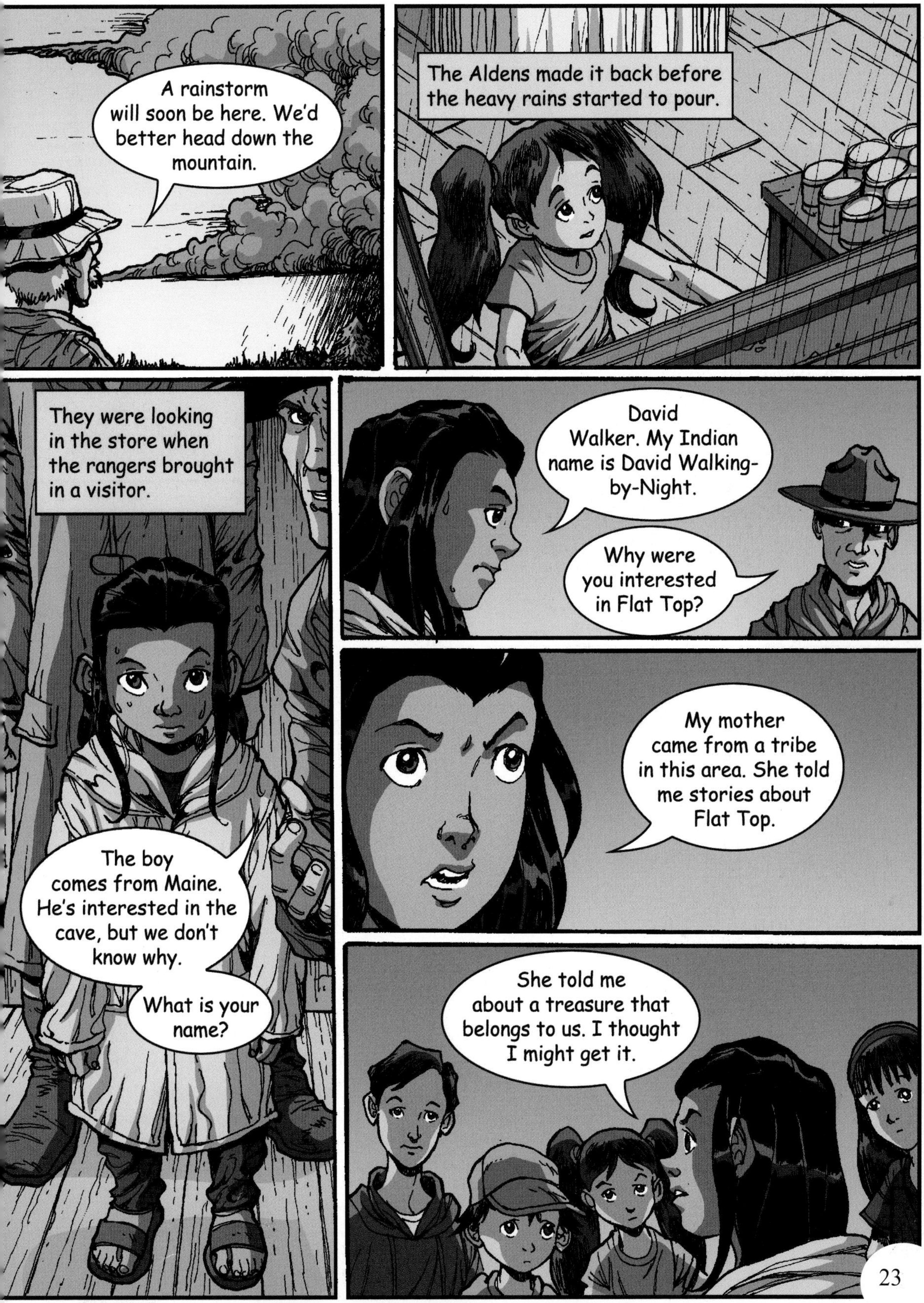
A rainstorm will soon be here. We'd better head down the mountain.
The Aldens made it back before the heavy rains started to pour.
They were looking in the store when the rangers brought in a visitor.
The boy comes from Maine. He's interested in the cave, but we don't know why.
What is your name?
David Walker. My Indian name is David Walking-by-Night.
Why were you interested in Flat Top?
My mother came from a tribe in this area. She told me stories about Flat Top.
She told me about a treasure that belongs to us. I thought I might get it.

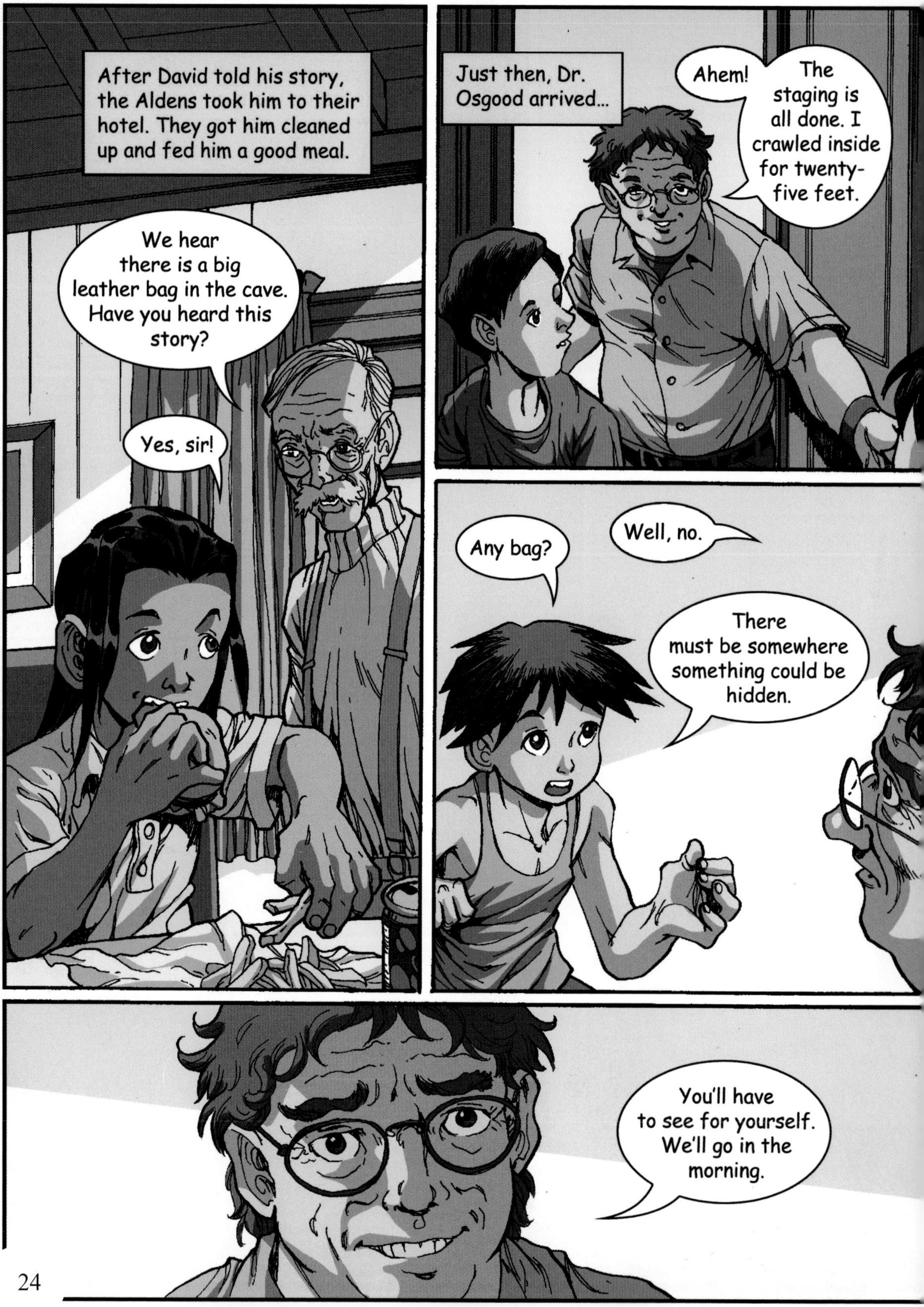
After David told his story, the Aldens took him to their hotel. They got him cleaned up and fed him a good meal.
We hear there is a big leather bag in the cave. Have you heard this story?
Yes, sir!
Just then, Dr. Osgood arrived...
Ahem!
The staging is all done. I crawled inside for twenty-five feet.
Any bag?
Well, no.
There must be somewhere something could be hidden.
You'll have to see for yourself. We'll go in the morning.

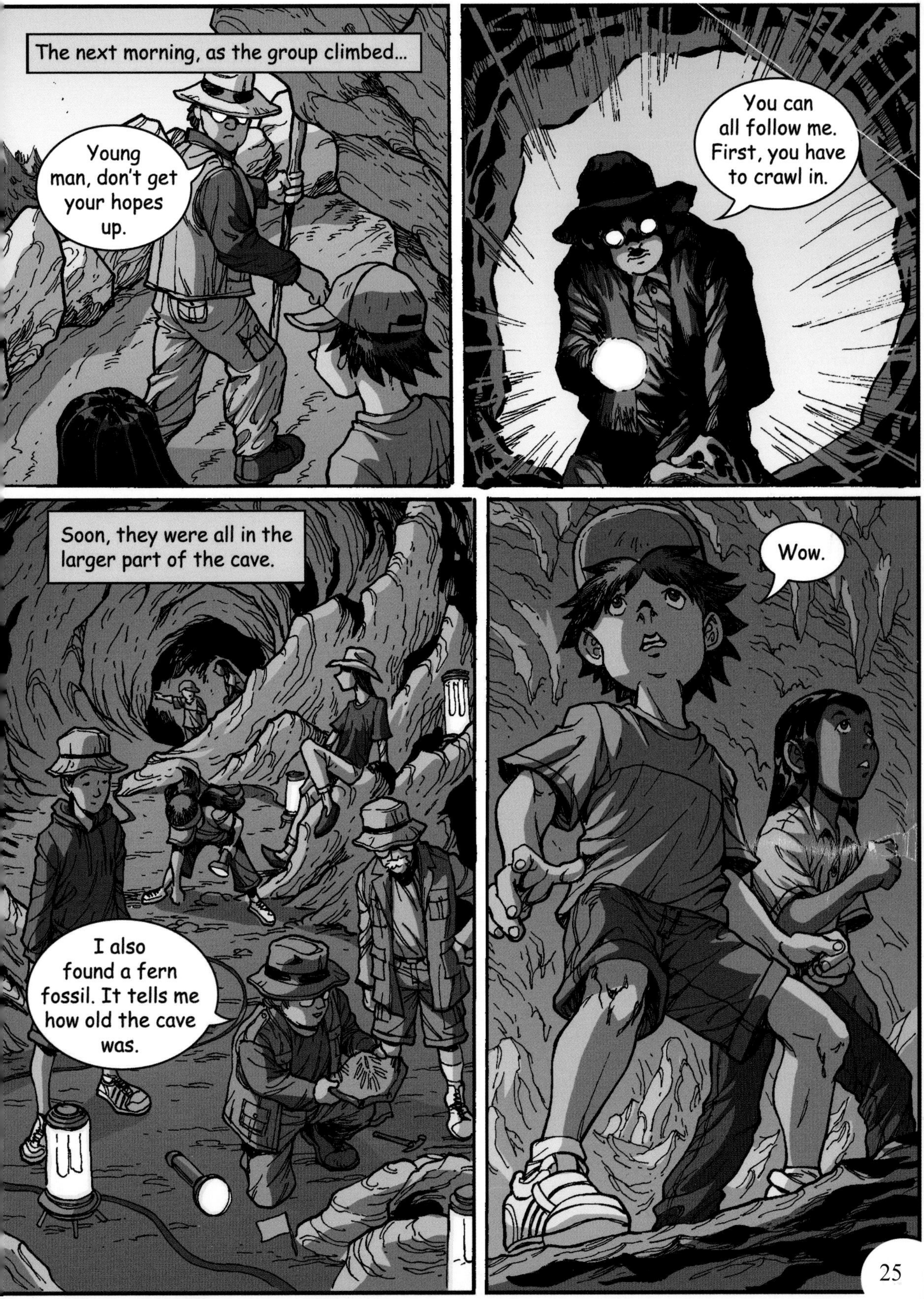
The next morning, as the group climbed...
Young man, don't get your hopes up.
You can all follow me. First, you have to crawl in.
Soon, they were all in the larger part of the cave.
I also found a fern fossil. It tells me how old the cave was.
Wow.

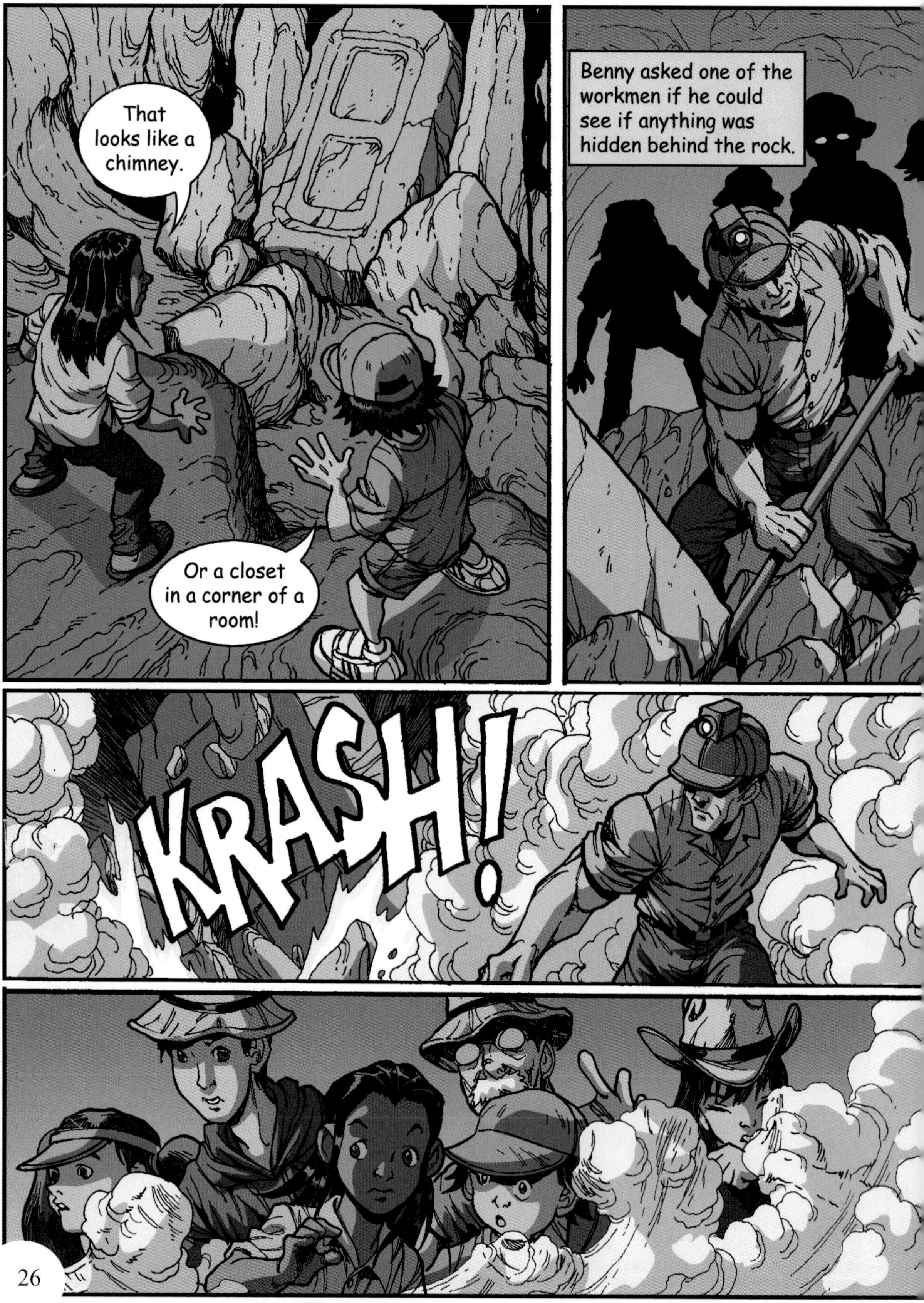
That looks like a chimney.
Or a closet in a corner of a room!
Benny asked one of the workmen if he could see if anything was hidden behind the rock.
KRASH!

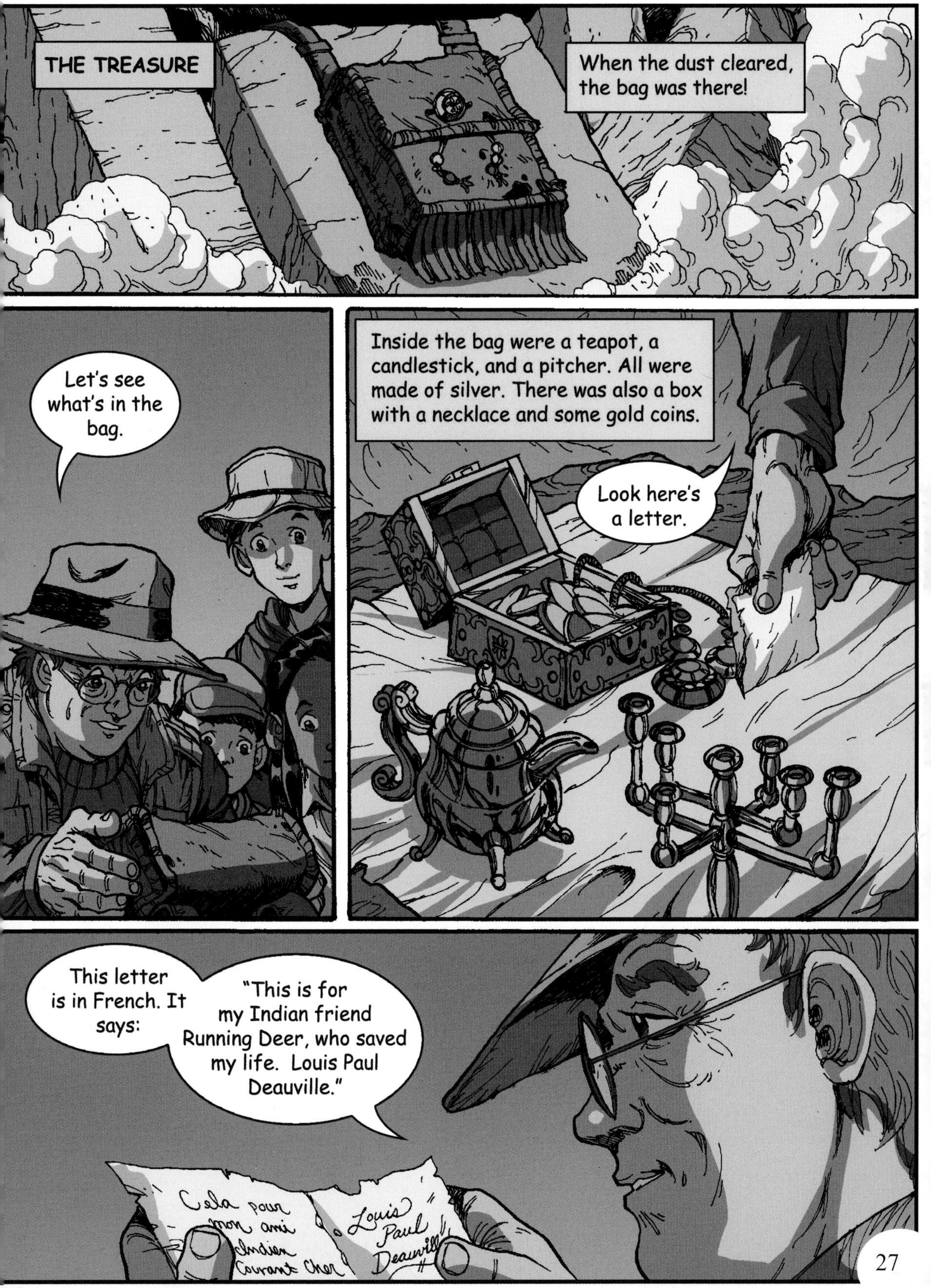
THE TREASURE
When the dust cleared, the bag was there!
Let's see what's in the bag.
Inside the bag were a teapot, a candlestick, and a pitcher. All were made of silver. There was also a box with a necklace and some gold coins.
Look here's a letter.
This letter is in French. It says:
"This is for my Indian friend Running Deer, who saved my life. Louis Paul Deauville."
Cela pour mon ami Indien Courant Cher
Louis Paul Deauvill

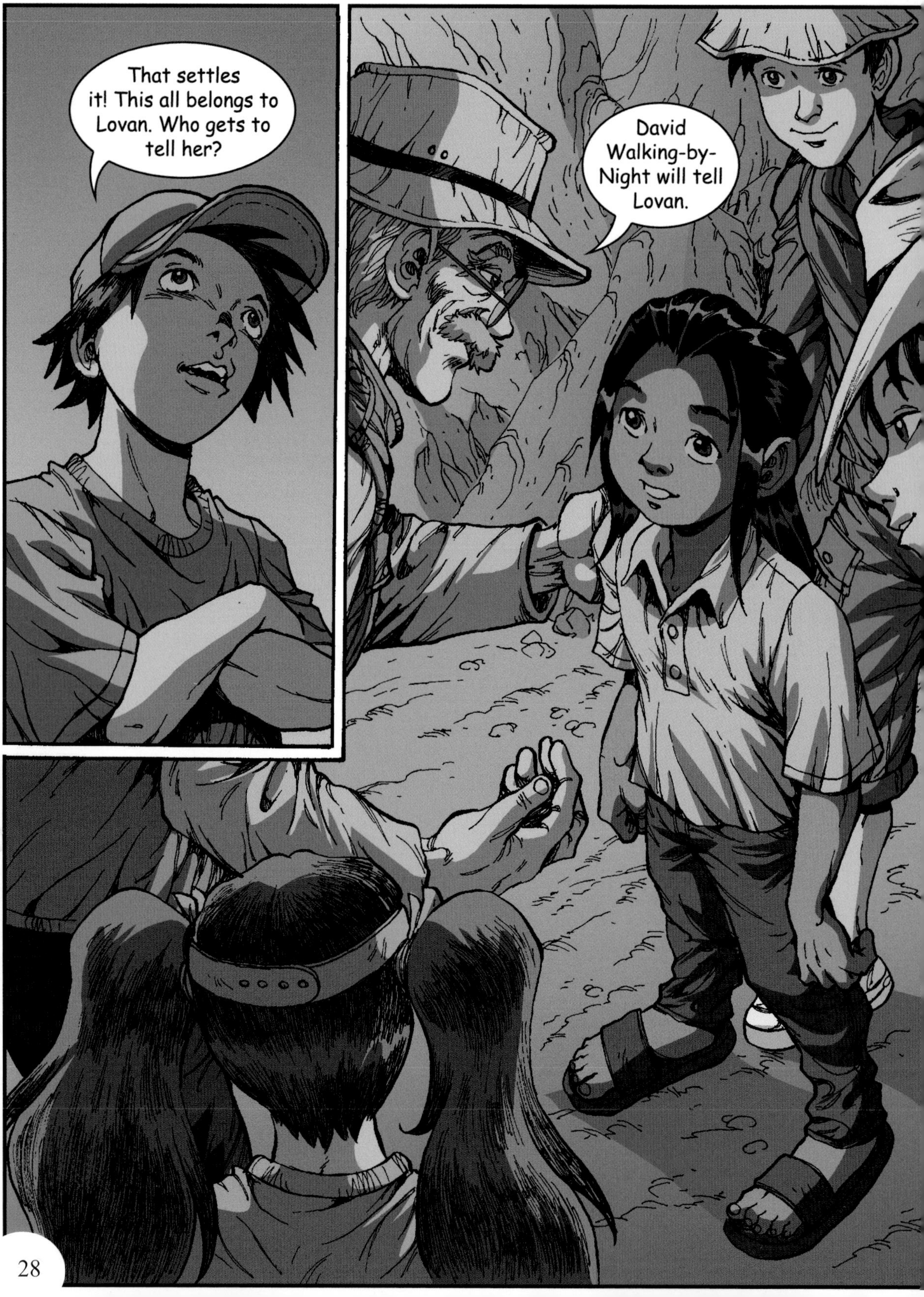
That settles it! This all belongs to Lovan. Who gets to tell her?
David Walking-by-Night will tell Lovan.

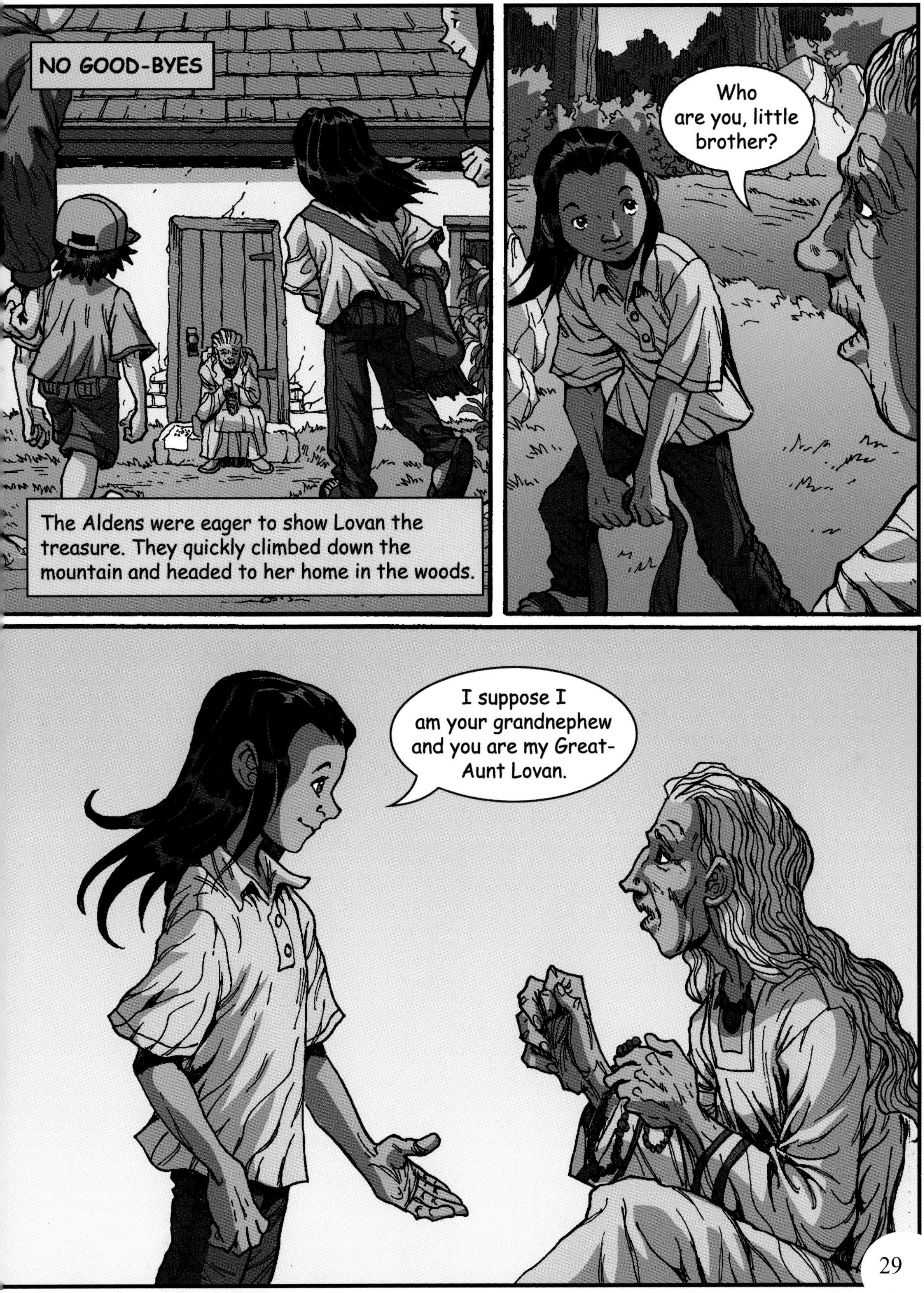
NO GOOD-BYES
The Aldens were eager to show Lovan the treasure. They quickly climbed down the mountain and headed to her home in the woods.
Who are you, little brother?
I suppose I am your grandnephew and you are my Great-Aunt Lovan.

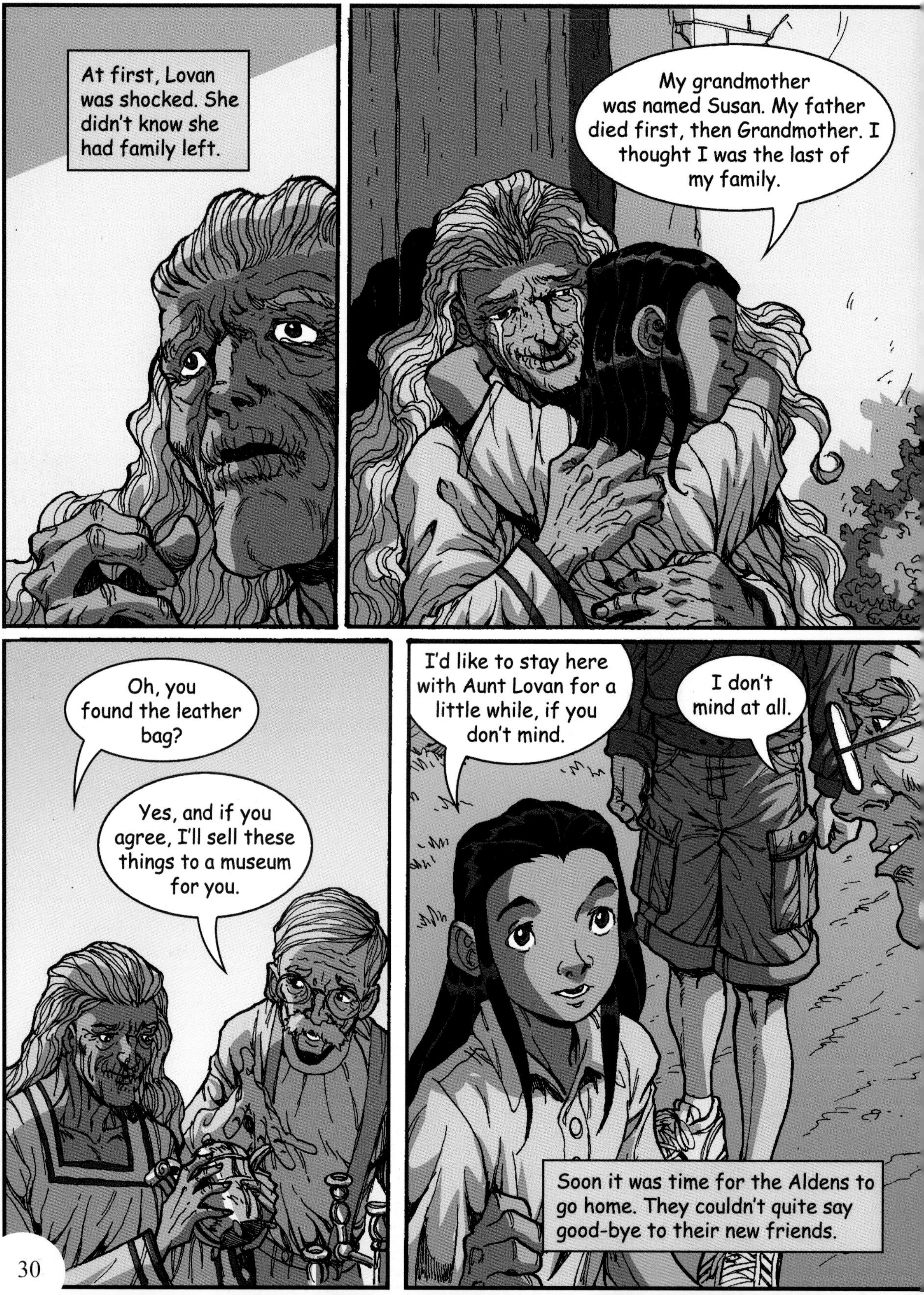

At first, Lovan was shocked. She didn't know she had family left.
My grandmother was named Susan. My father died first, then Grandmother. I thought I was the last of my family.
Oh, you found the leather bag?
Yes, and if you agree, I'll sell these things to a museum for you.
I'd like to stay here with Aunt Lovan for a little while, if you don't mind.
I don't mind at all.
Soon it was time for the Aldens to go home. They couldn't quite say good-bye to their new friends.

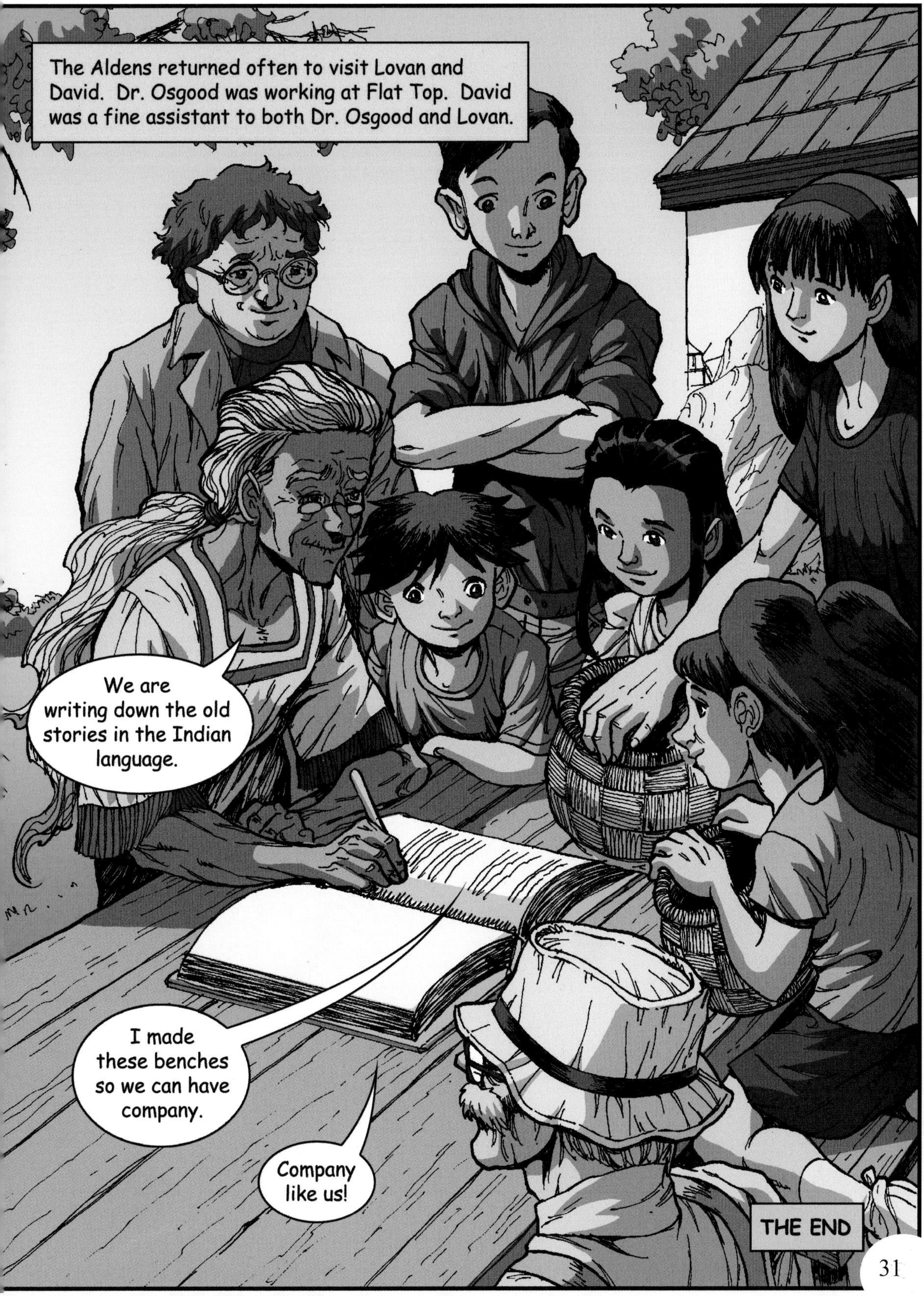

The Aldens returned often to visit Lovan and David. Dr. Osgood was working at Flat Top. David was a fine assistant to both Dr. Osgood and Lovan.
We are writing down the old stories in the Indian language.
I made these benches so we can have company.
Company like us!
THE END

# ABOUT THE CREATOR

Gertrude Chandler Warner was born on April 16, 1890, in Putnam, Connecticut. In 1918, Warner began teaching at Israel Putnam School. As a teacher, she discovered that many readers who liked an exciting story could not find books that were both easy and fun to read. She decided to try to meet this need. In 1942, *The Boxcar Children* was published for these readers.

Warner drew on her own experience to write *The Boxcar Children*. As a child she spent hours watching trains go by on the tracks near her family home. She often dreamed about what it would be like to live in a caboose or freight car—just as the Alden children do.

When readers asked for more Alden adventures, Warner began additional stories. While the mystery element is central to each of the books, she never thought of them as strictly juvenile mysteries. She liked to stress the Aldens' independence. Henry, Jessie, Violet, and Benny go about most of their adventures with as little adult supervision as possible—something that delights young readers.

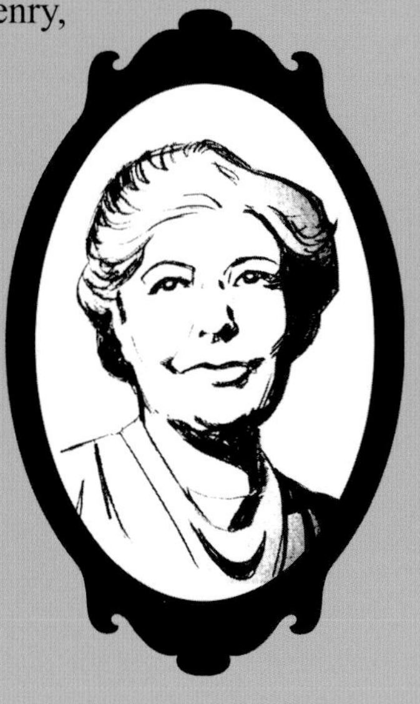

During her lifetime, Warner received hundreds of letters from fans as she continued the Aldens' adventures, writing nineteen Boxcar Children books in all. After her death in 1979, her publisher, Albert Whitman and Company, carried on Warner's vision. Today, the Boxcar Children series has more than 100 books.